A WORDLESS GRAPHIC NOVEL

# PICNIC PIGS

by Derek Fridolfs
illustrated by Scott Gross

PICTURE WINDOW BOOKS
a capstone imprint

Published by Picture Window Books,
an imprint of Capstone
1710 Roe Crest Drive
North Mankato, Minnesota 56003
capstonepub.com

Library of Congress Cataloging-in-Publication Data
Names: Fridolfs, Derek, author. | Gross, Scott, illustrator.
Title: Picnic pigs / by Derek Fridolfs ; illustrated by Scott Gross.
   Other titles: Looney Tunes.
Description: North Mankato, Minnesota : Picture Window Books, an
   imprint of Capstone [2021] | Series: Looney Tunes wordless
   graphic novels | Audience: Ages 5-7. | Audience: Grades K-2. |
   Summary: "As Porky and Petunia settle in for a picnic in the park,
   nature crashes their party. Can Porky overcome the elements in
   time to get some cake and eat it too?"—Provided by publisher.
Identifiers: LCCN 2021002774 (print) | LCCN 2021002775 (ebook)
   | ISBN 9781663910103 (hardcover) | ISBN 9781663920331
   (paperback) | ISBN 9781663910073 (ebook pdf)
Subjects: LCSH: Graphic novels. | CYAC: Graphic novels. | Stories
   without words. | Porky Pig (Fictitious character)--Fiction. |
   Picnics—Fiction.
Classification: LCC PZ7.7.F784 Pi 2021 (print) | LCC PZ7.7.F784
   (ebook) | DDC 741.5/973—dc23
LC record available at https://lccn.loc.gov/2021002774
LC ebook record available at https://lccn.loc.gov/2021002775

Designed by Dina Her

Printed and bound in the USA. 4270

# Meet

# PORKY AND PETUNIA

## Porky Pig

Porky Pig is a shy pig who has boundless energy and never gives up. He tries to live a happy-go-lucky life—even though sometimes the world seems to be out to get him. Porky may lose his cool in the midst of chaos, but his innocent charm and good intentions usually win out in the end.

## Petunia Pig

Petunia Pig has a cheerful and kind nature. As Porky's sweetheart, she is always happy to spend the day with him. Petunia also provides a good balance for Porky when he starts to lose his temper.

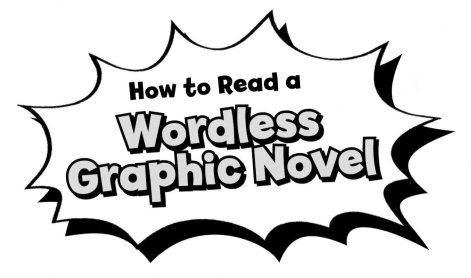

# How to Read a
## Wordless Graphic Novel

Wordless graphic novels are easy to read. Boxes called panels show you how to follow the story. Look at the panels from left to right and top to bottom. Read any sound effects as you go.

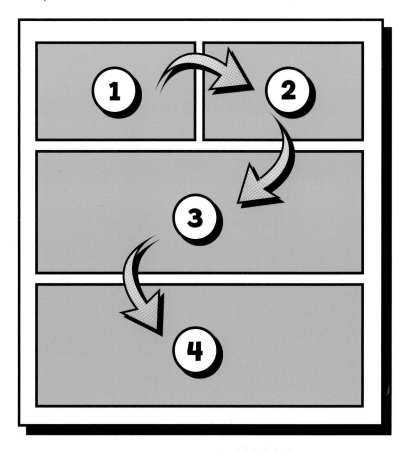

By putting the panels together, you'll understand the whole story!

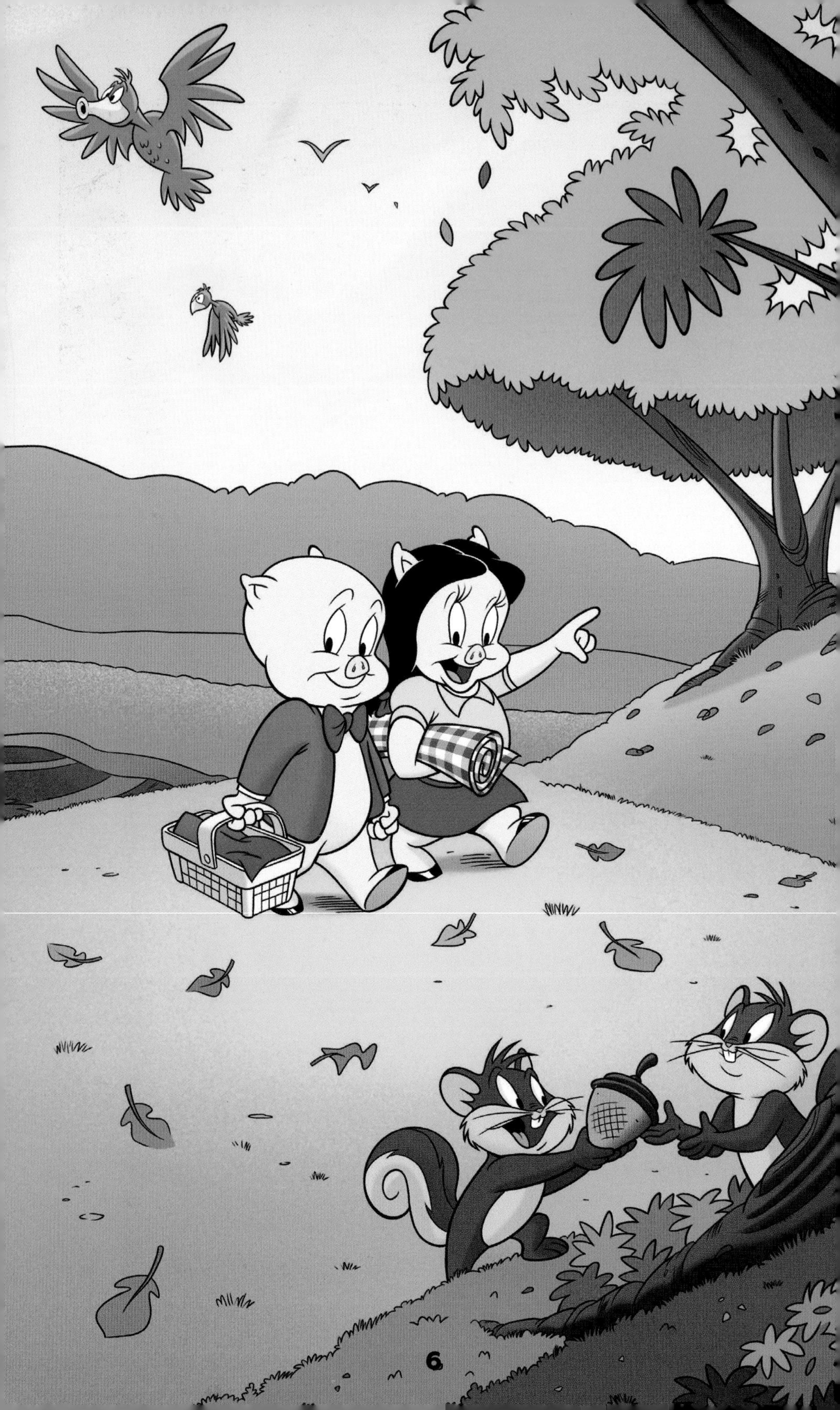

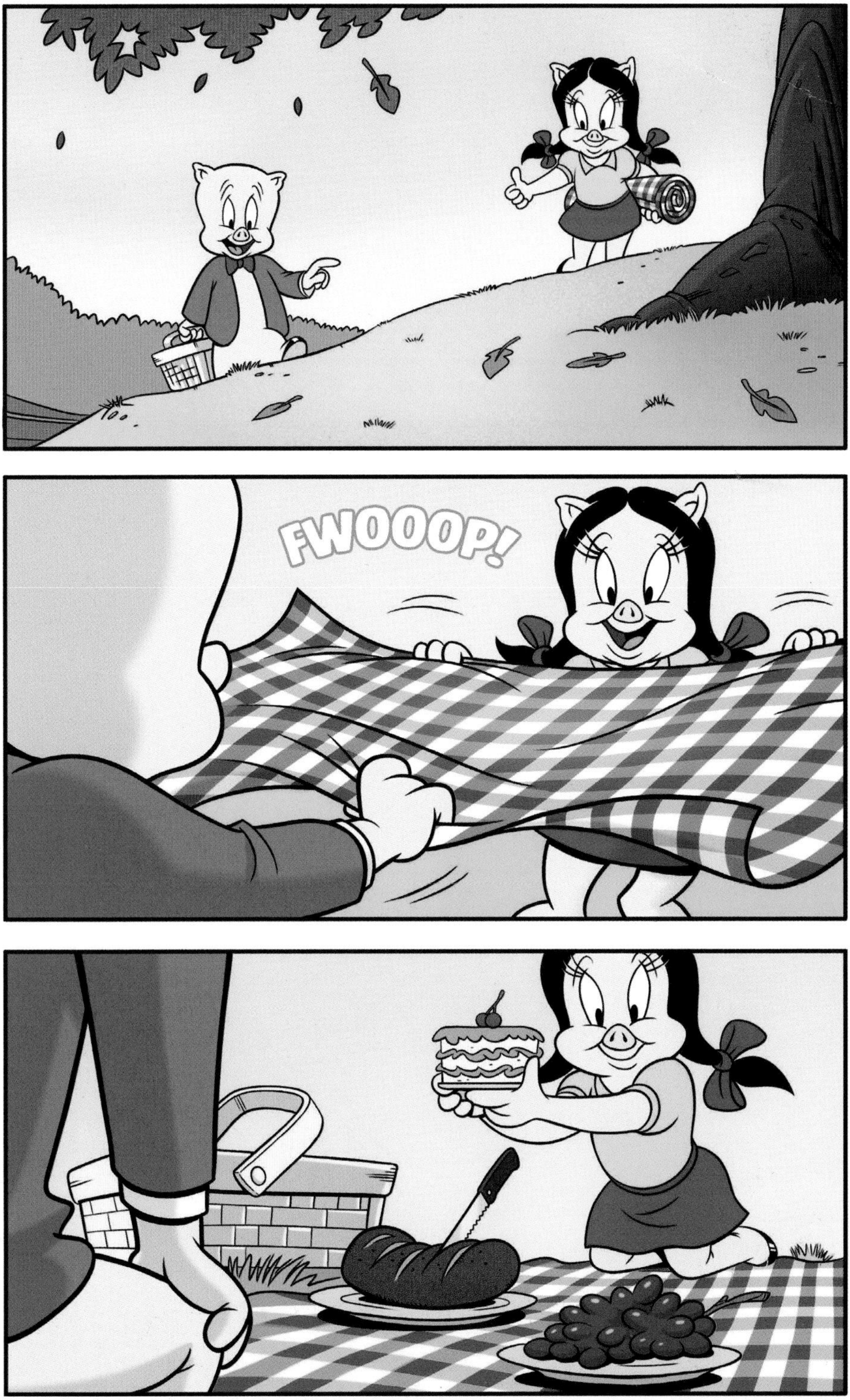
FWOOOP!

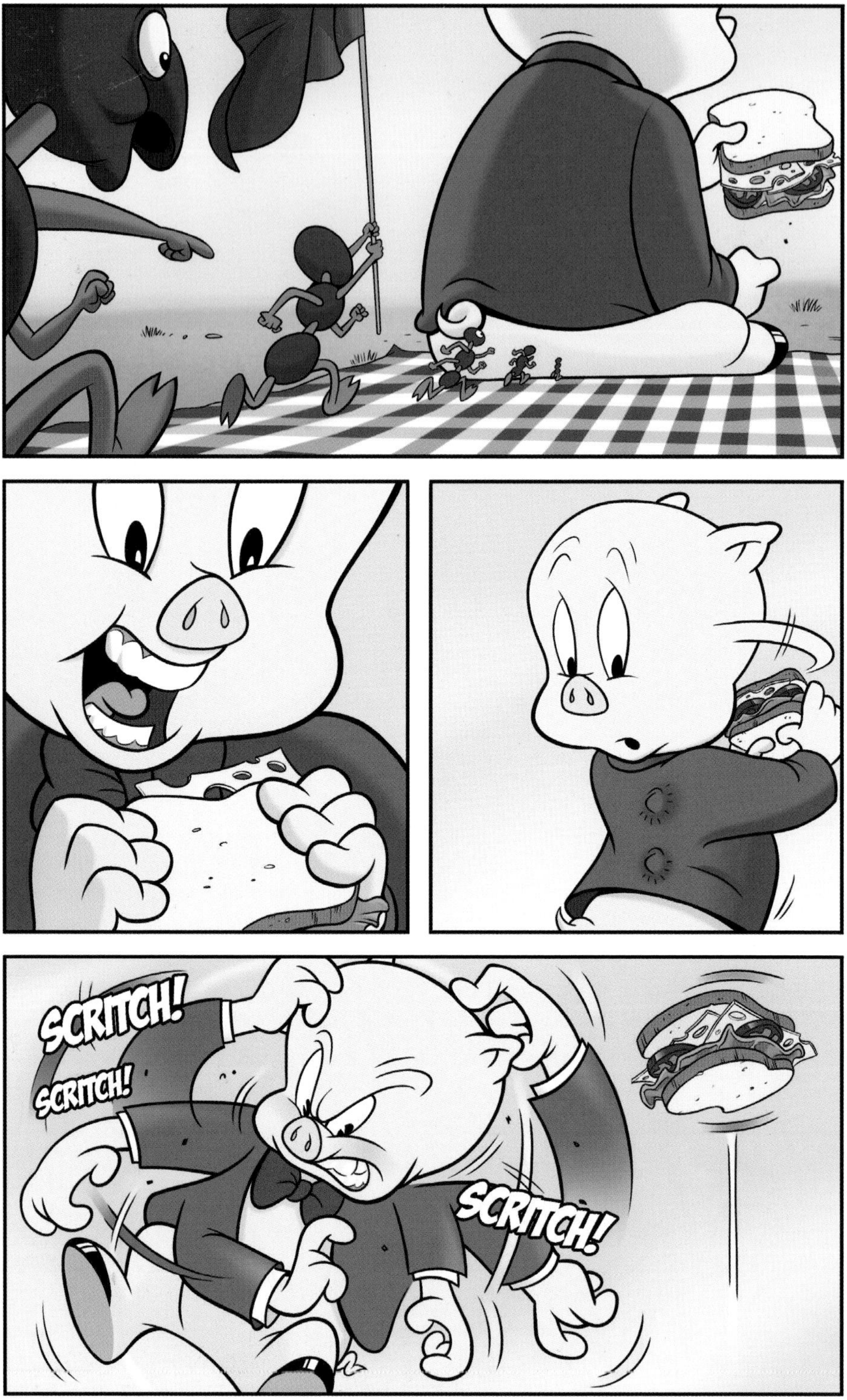
SCRITCH!
SCRITCH!
SCRITCH!

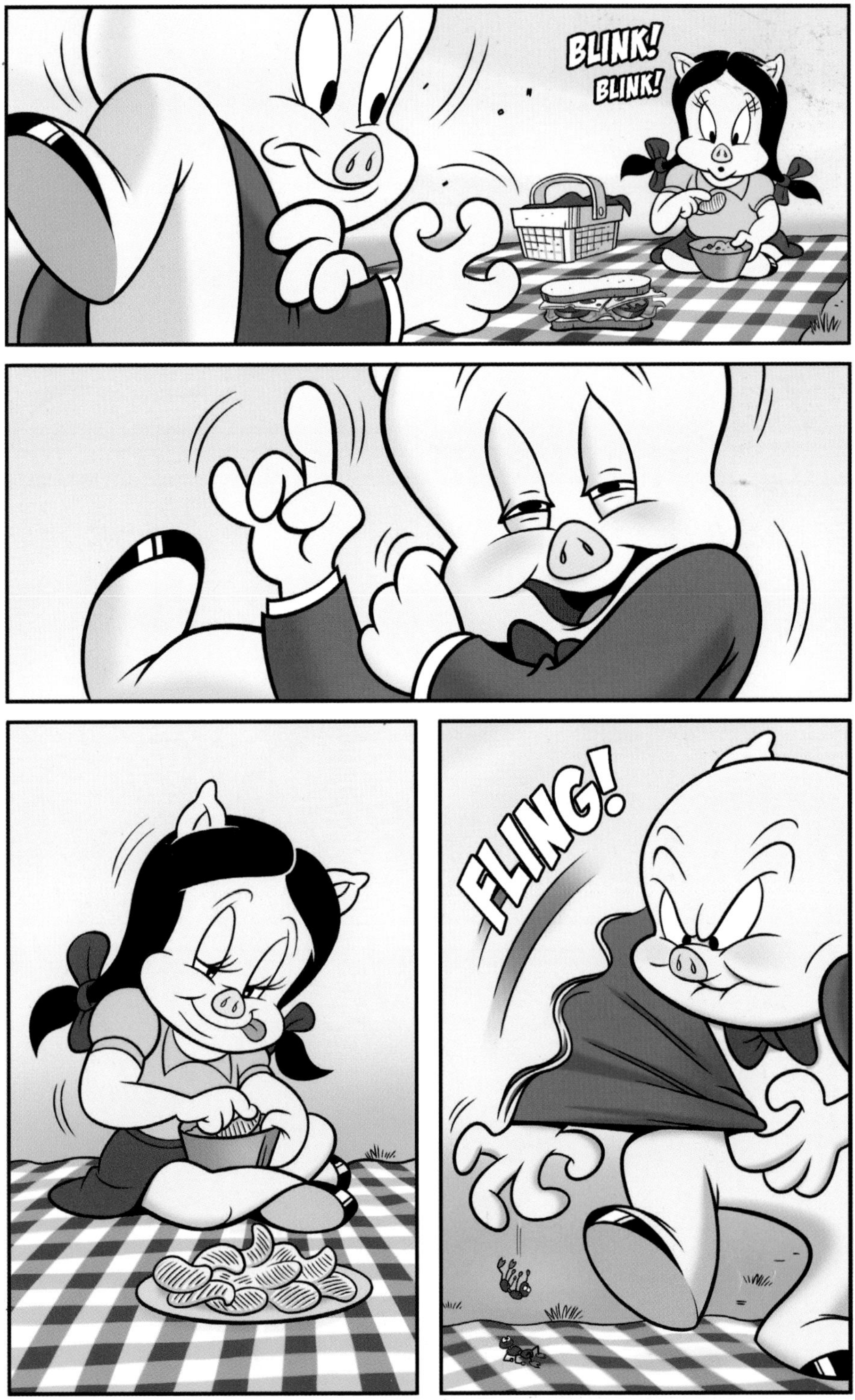
BLINK!
BLINK!
FLING!

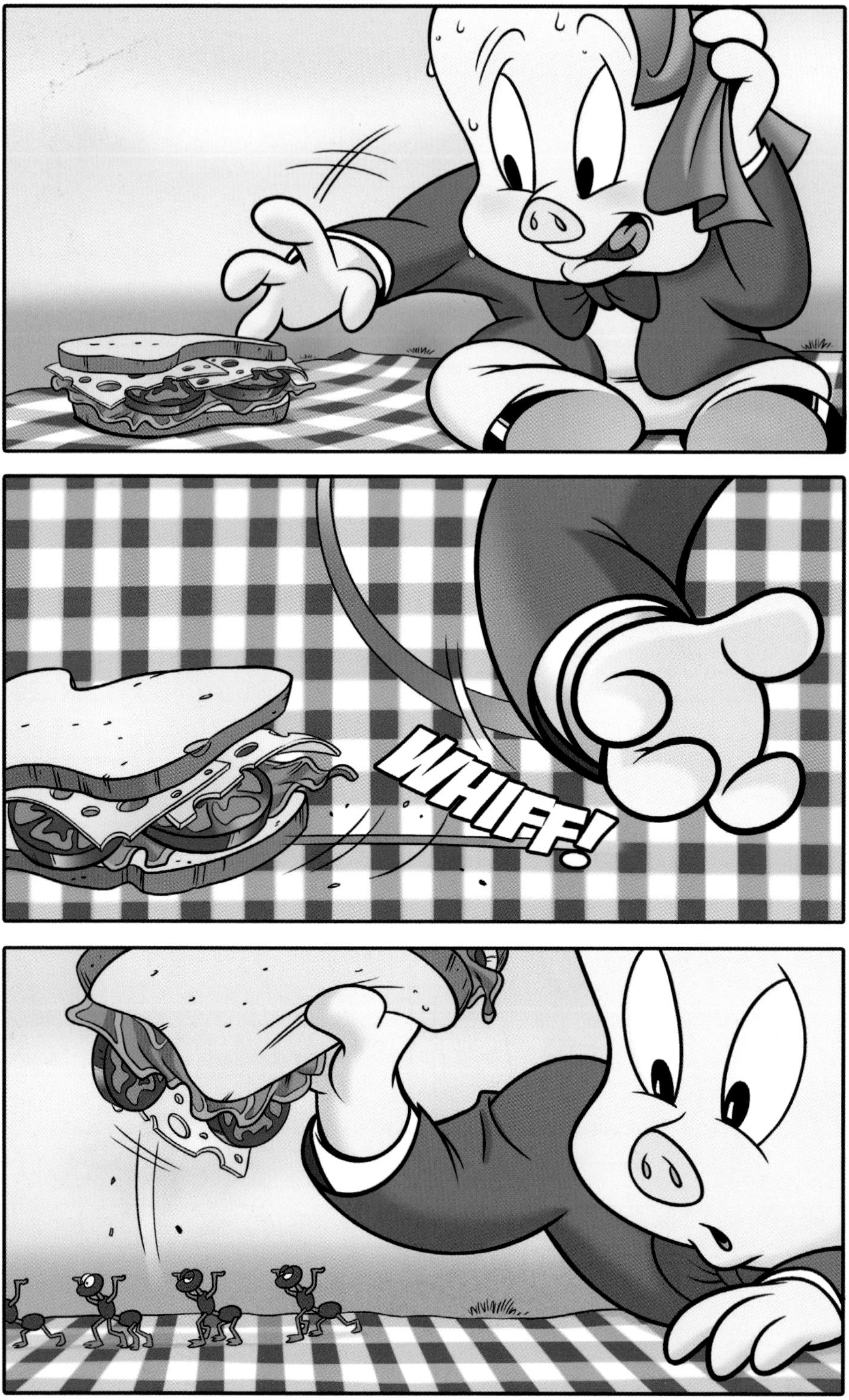
WHIFF!

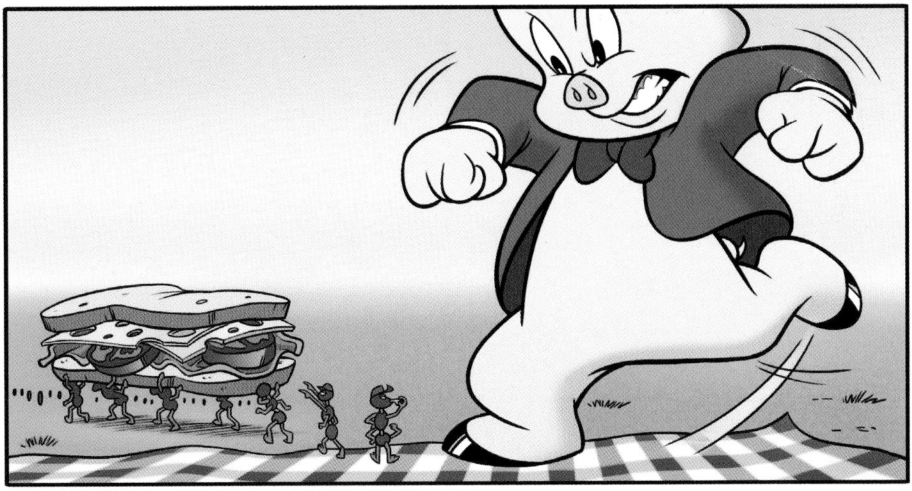

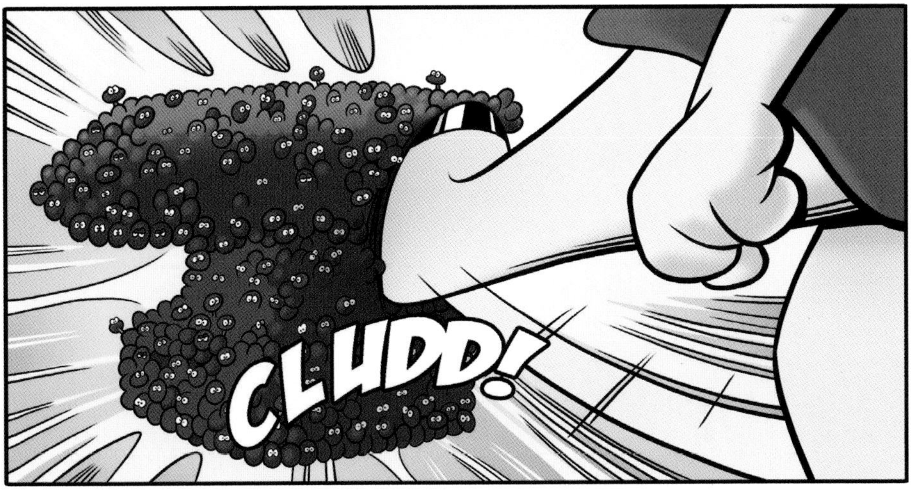
CLUDD!

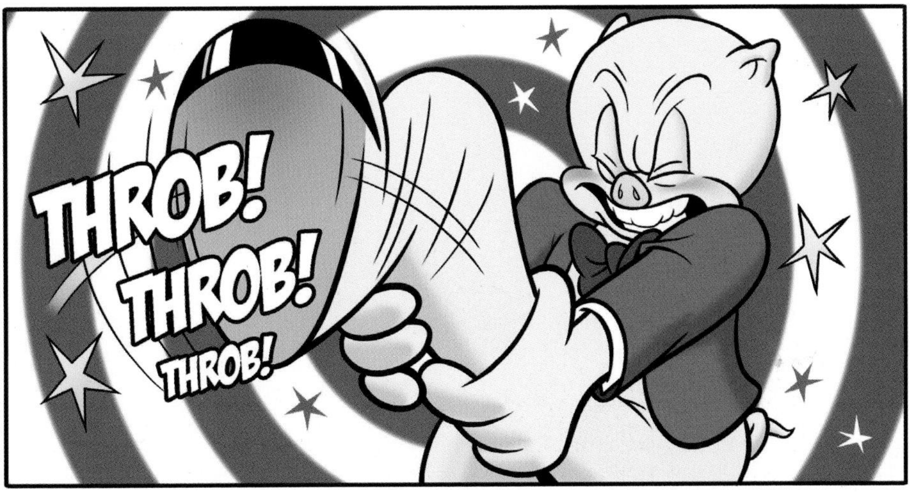
THROB!
THROB!
THROB!

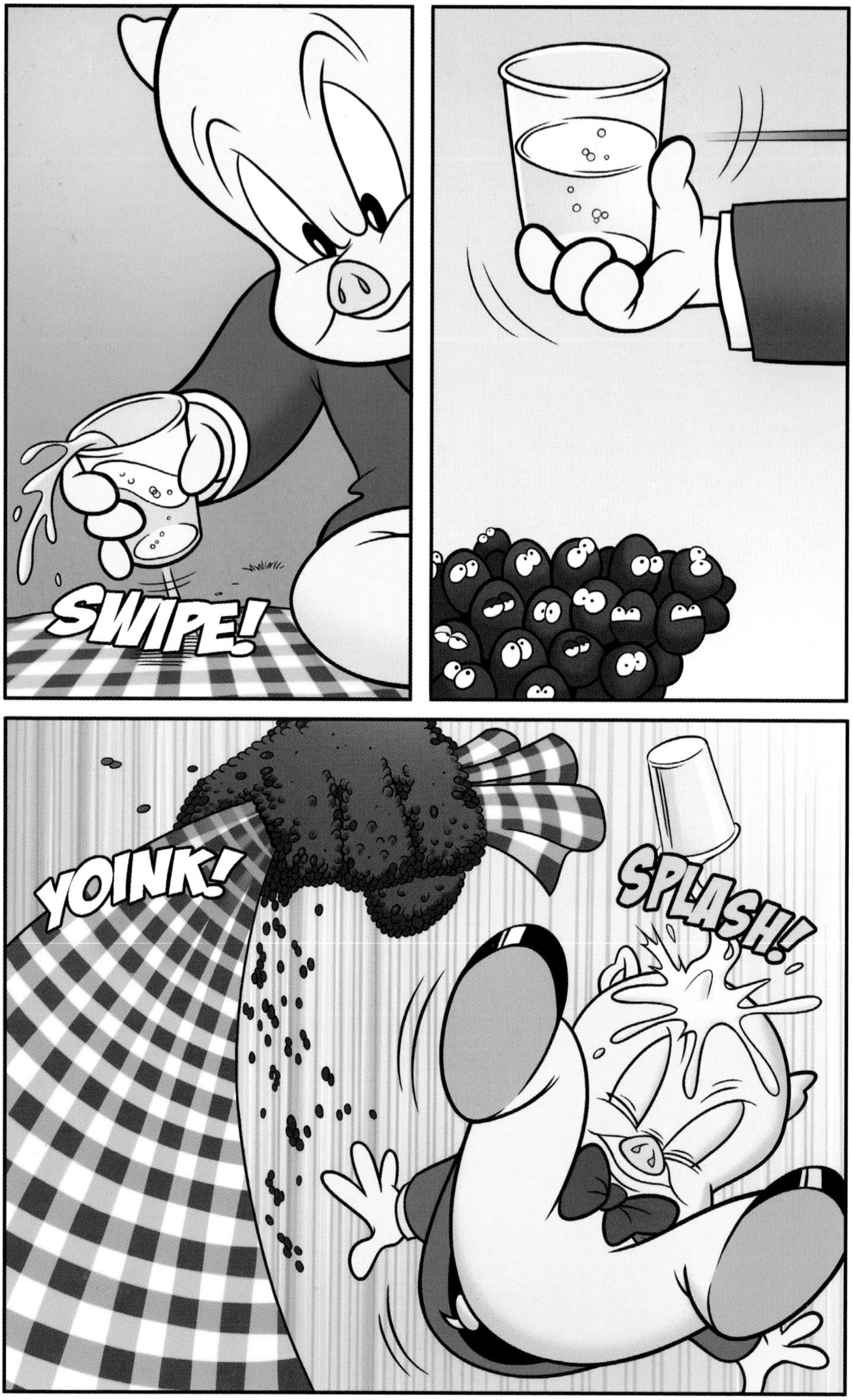
SWIPE!
YOINK!
SPLASH!

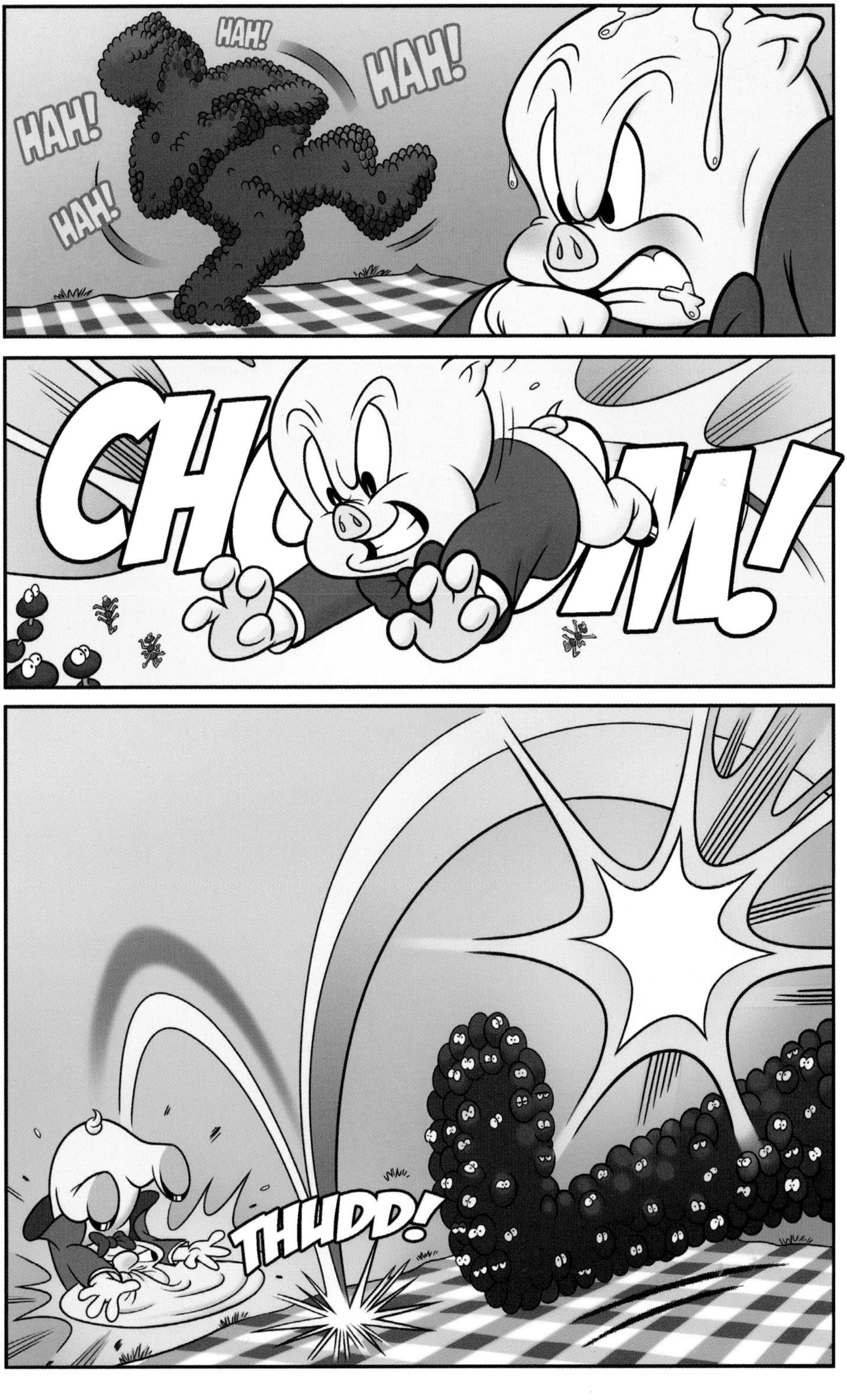
HAH!
HAH!
HAH!
HAH!
CH
M!
THUDD!

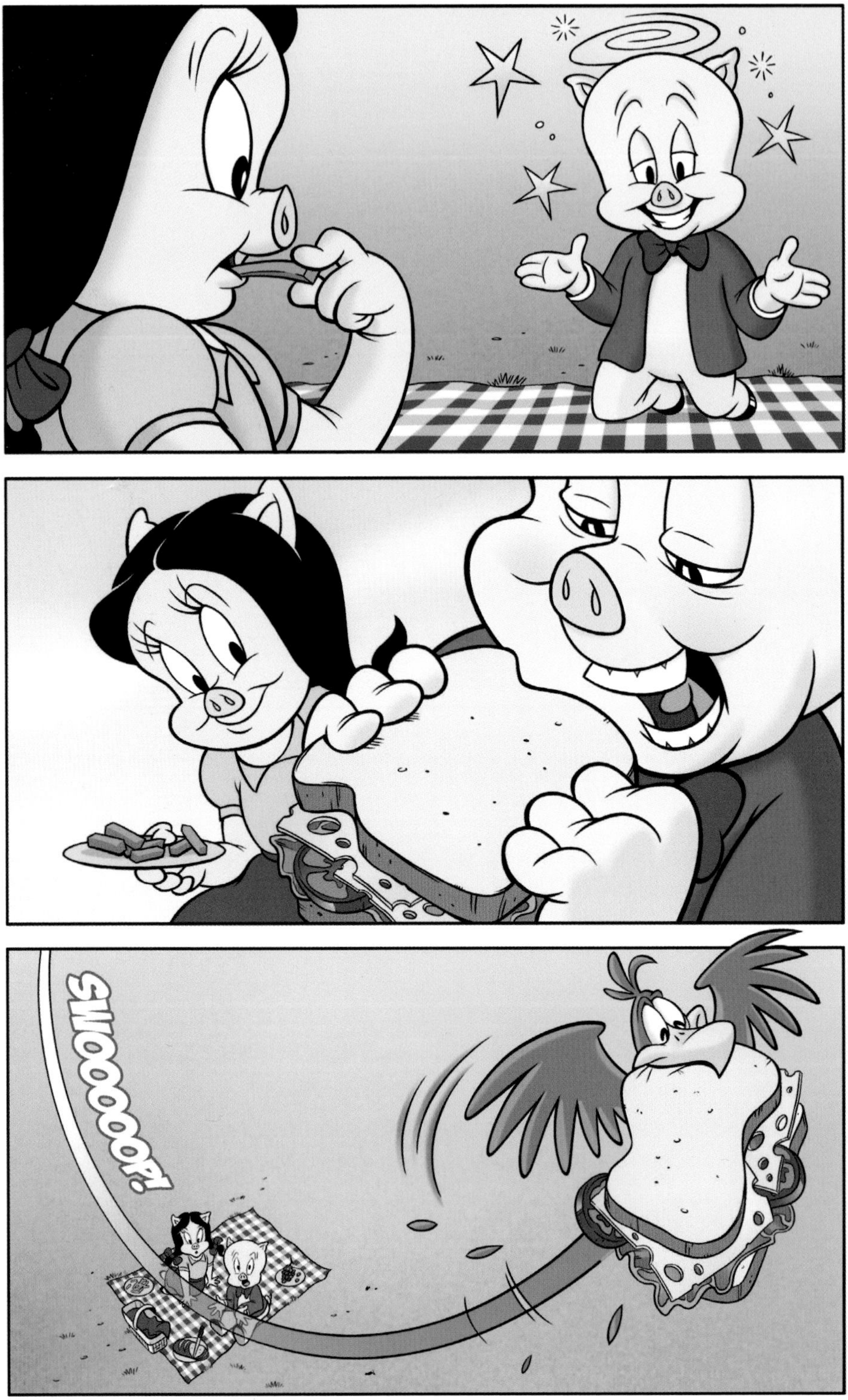
SWOOOOOOP!

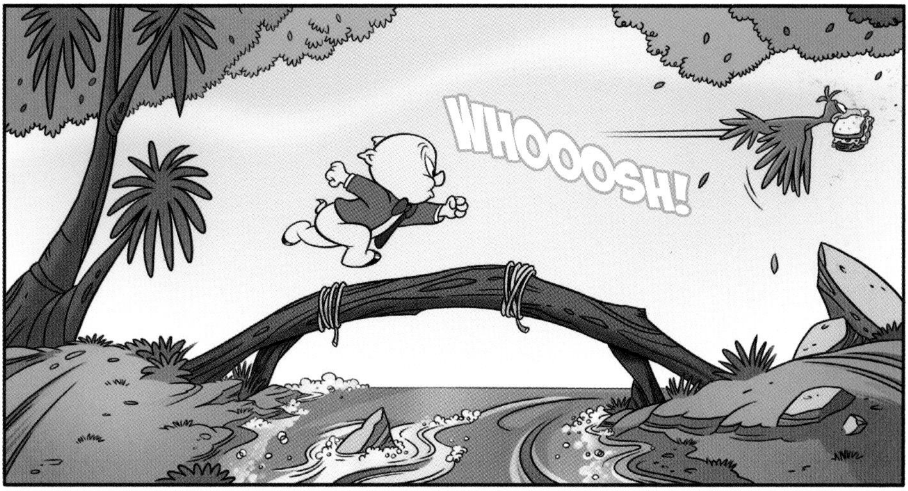
WHOOOOSH!

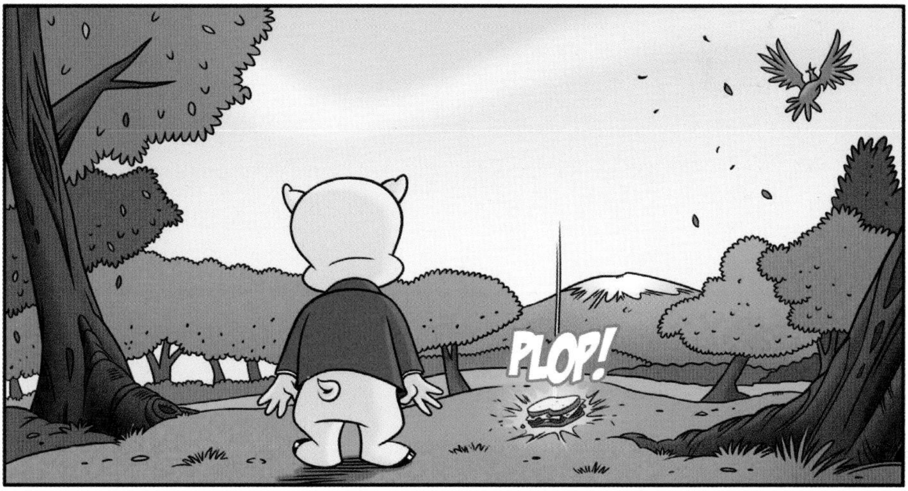
PLOP!

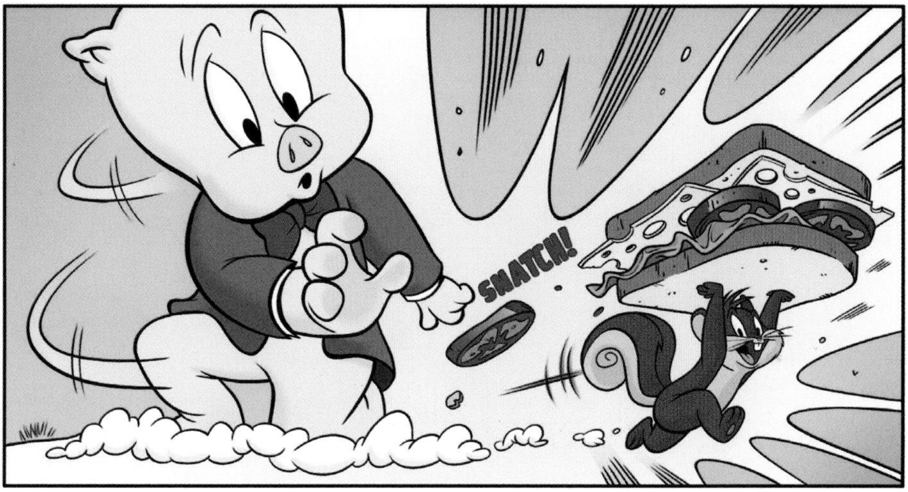
SNATCH!

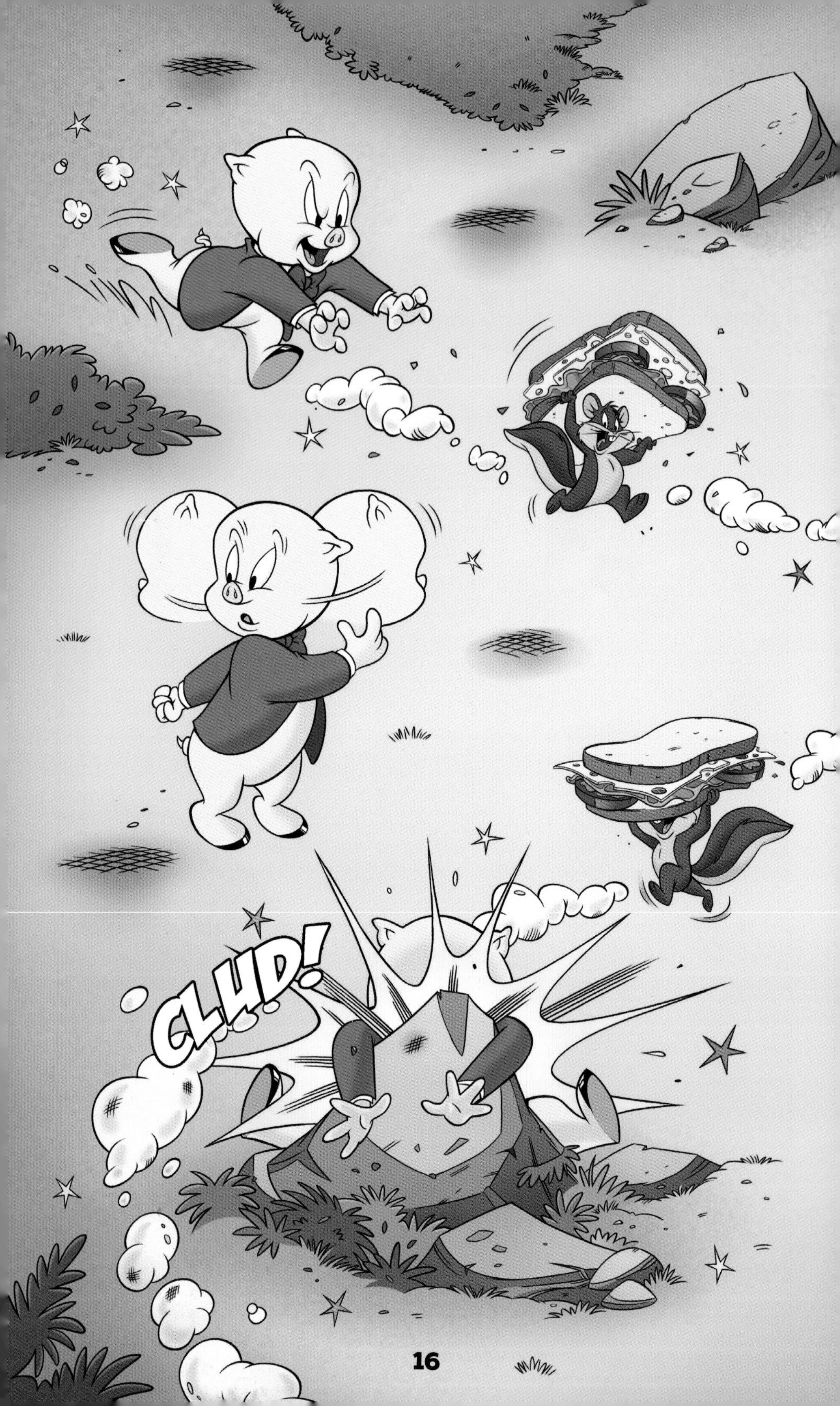
CLUD!

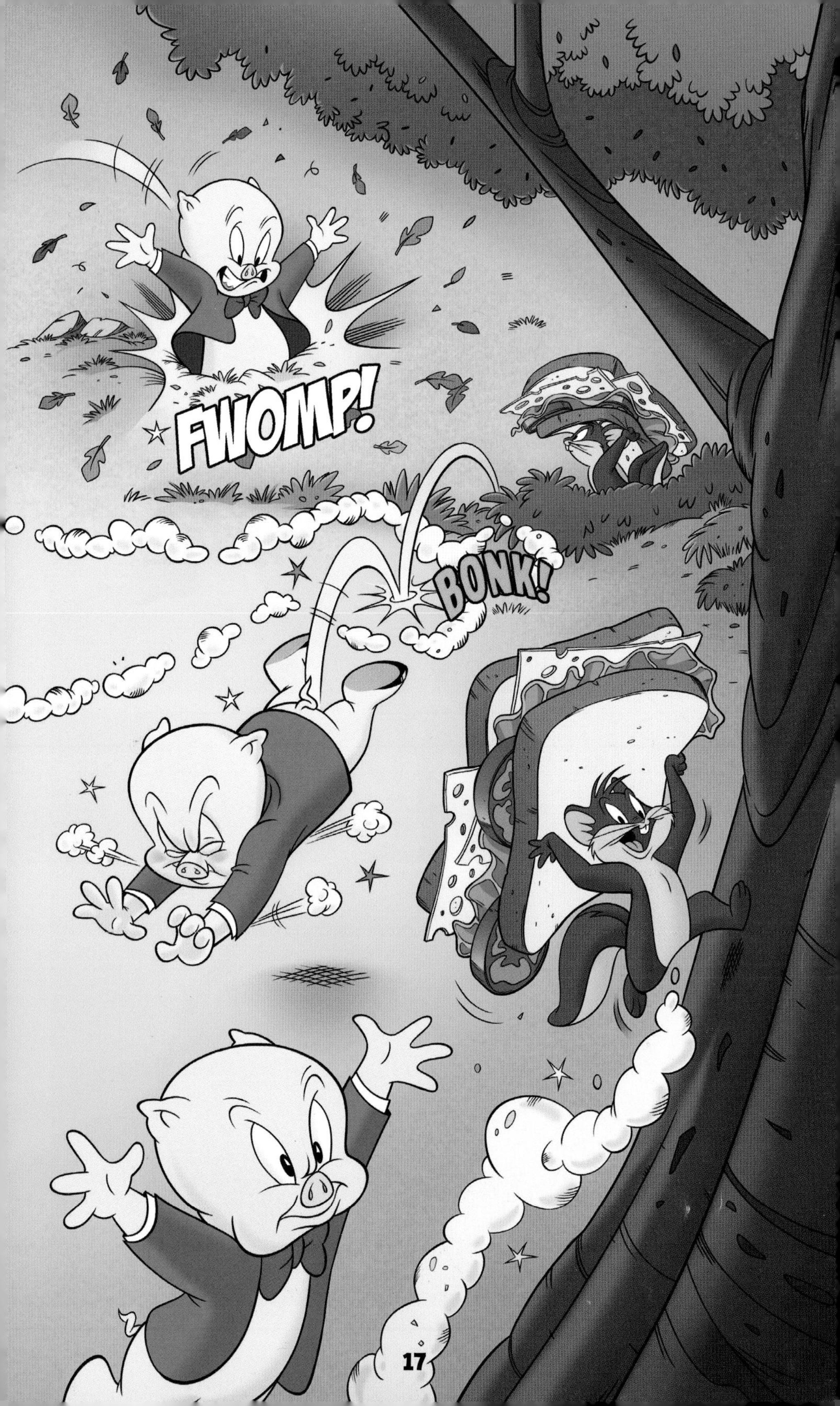
FWOMP!
BONK!

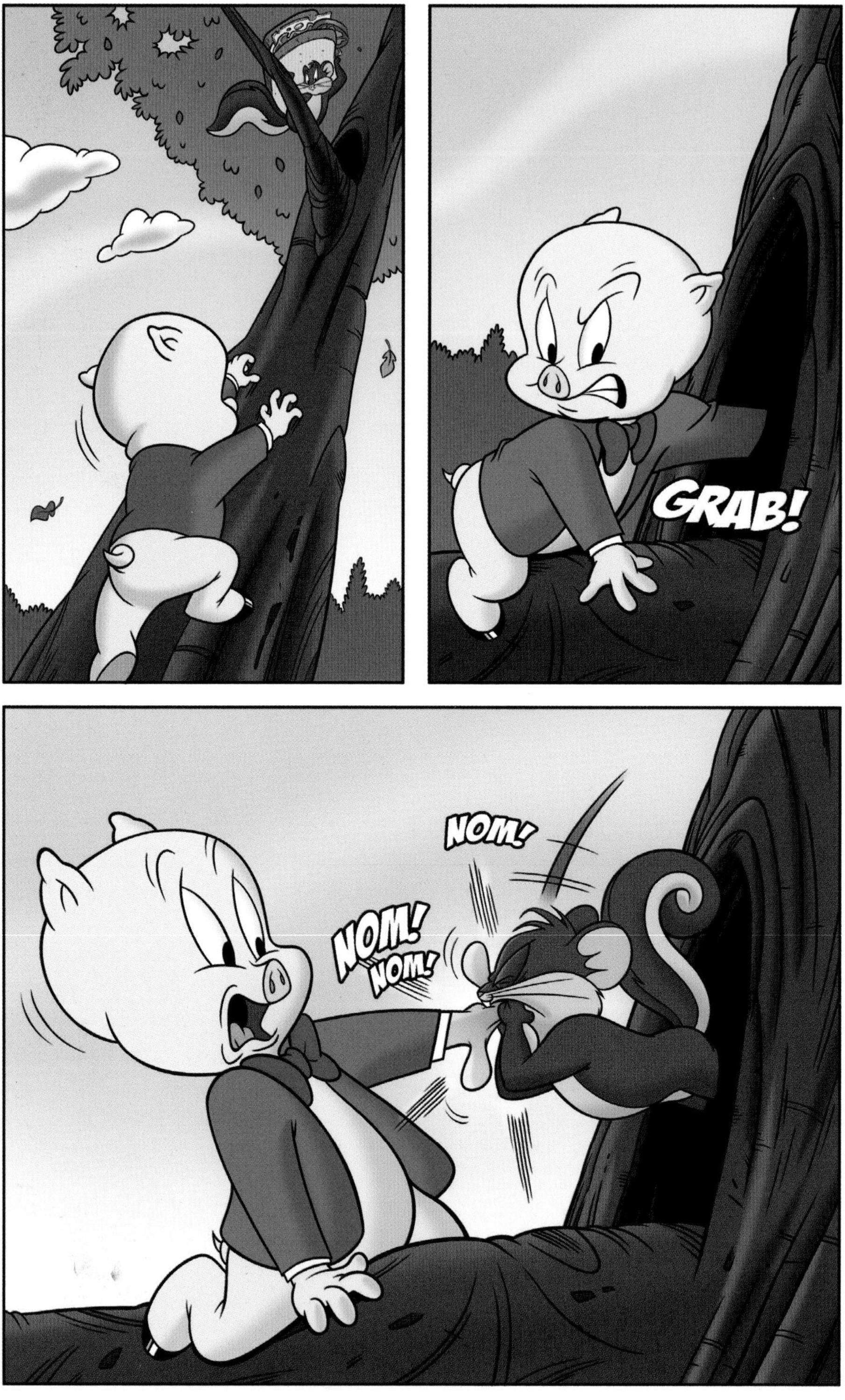

GRAB!
NOM!
NOM!
NOM!

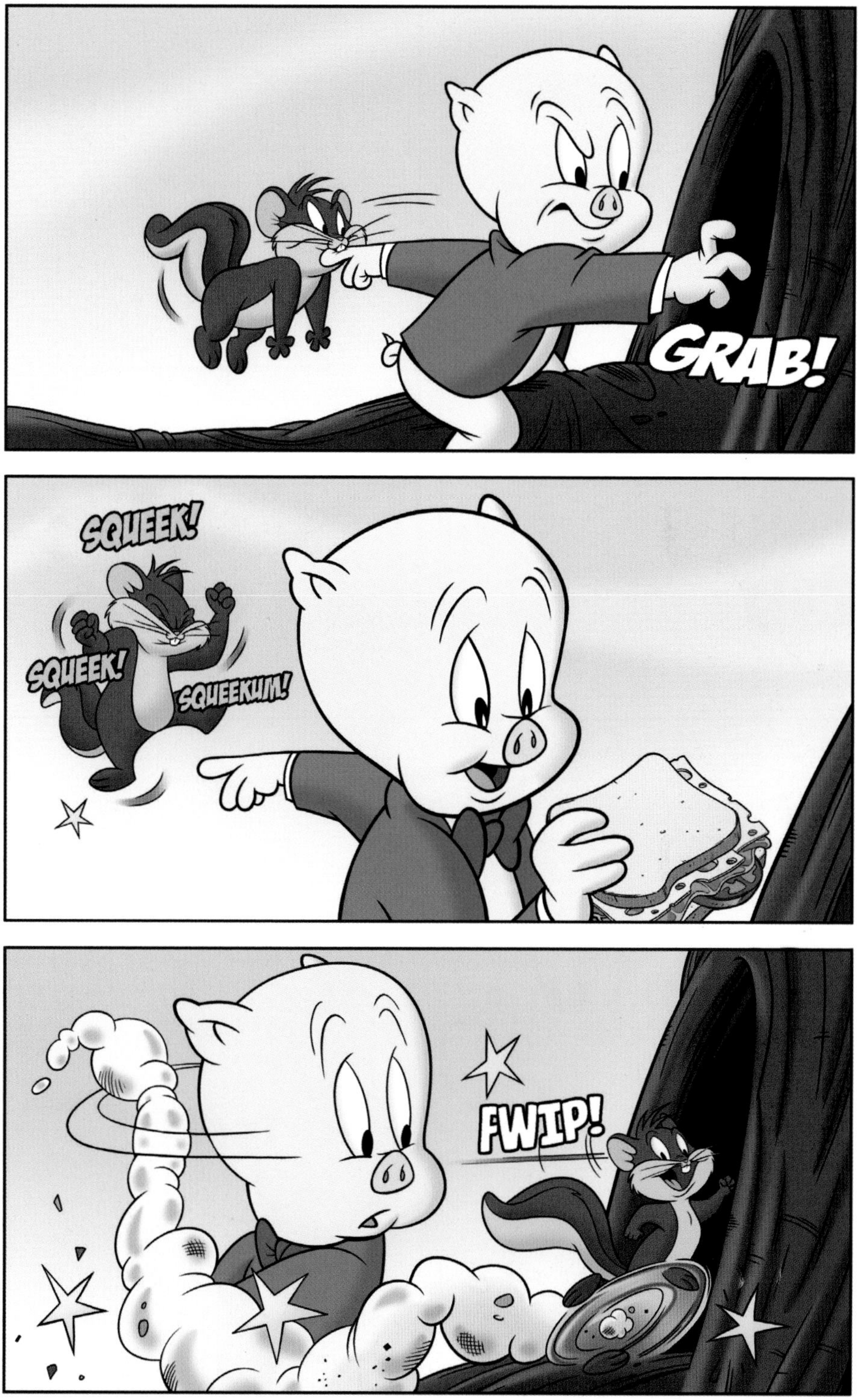
GRAB!
SQUEEK!
SQUEEK!
SQUEEKUM!
FWIP!

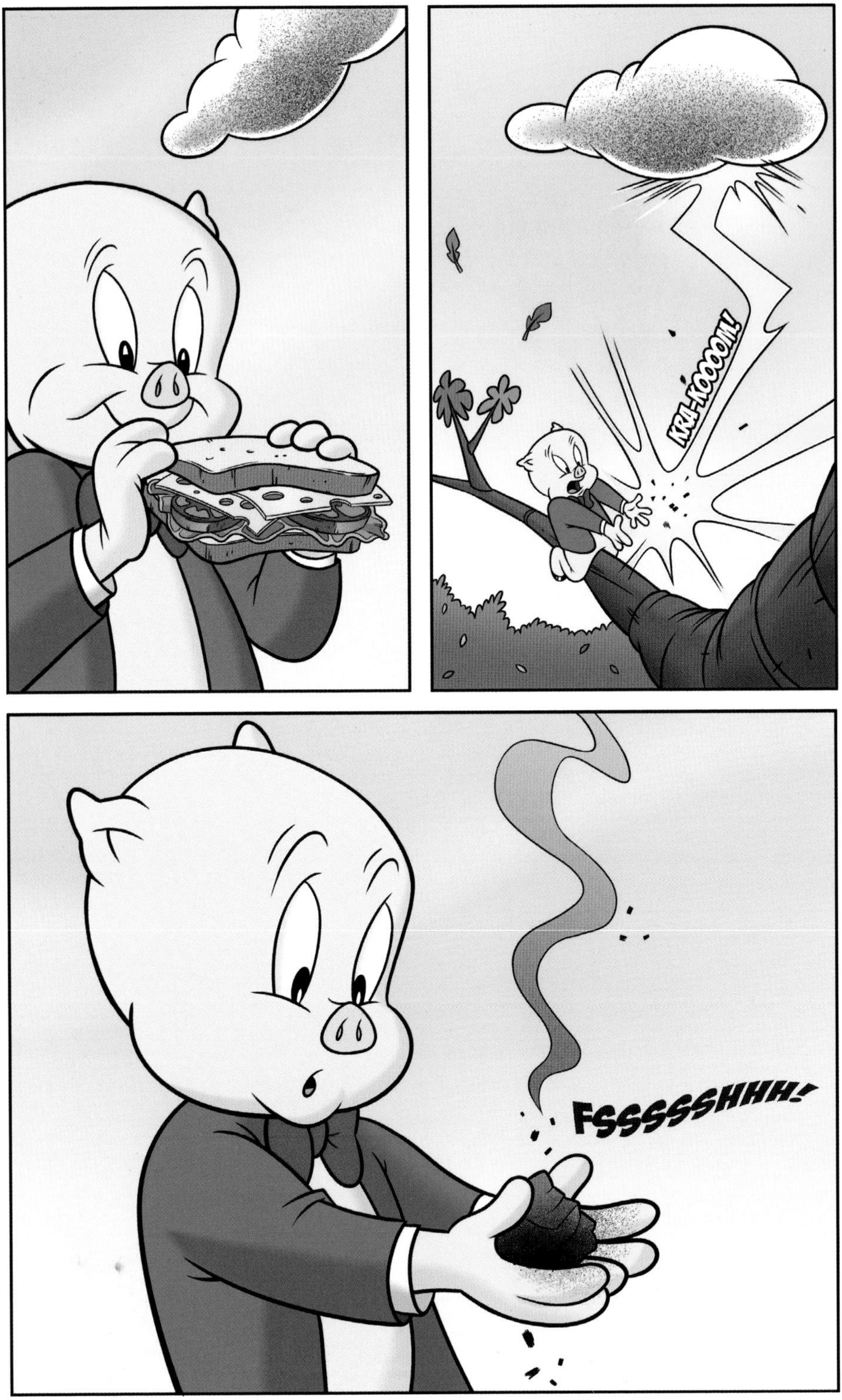
KRA-KOOOOM!
FSSSSSHHH!

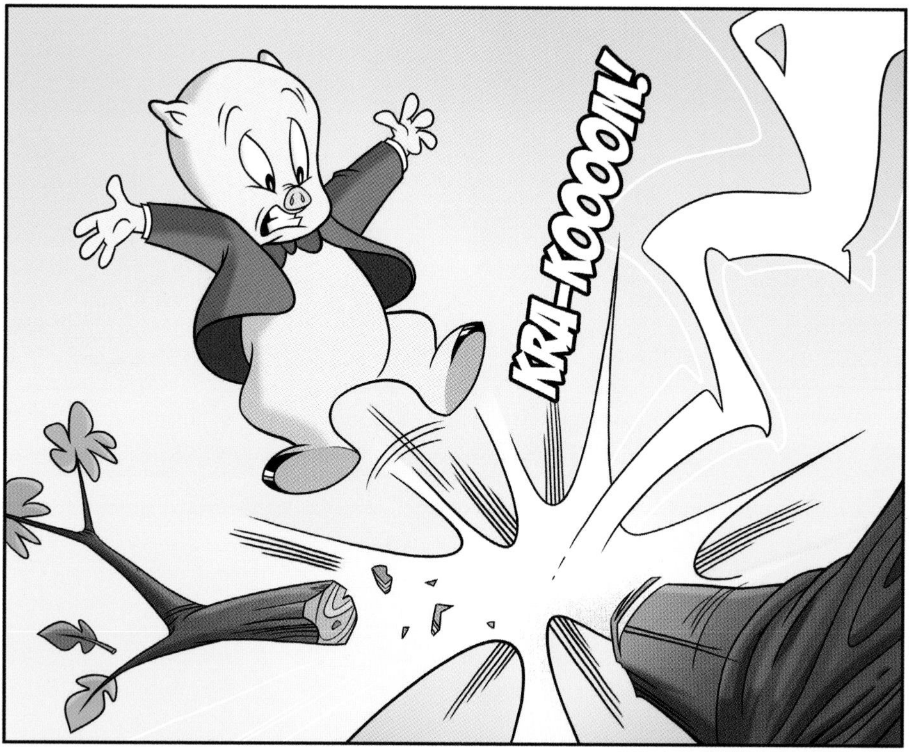
KRA-KOOOOM!

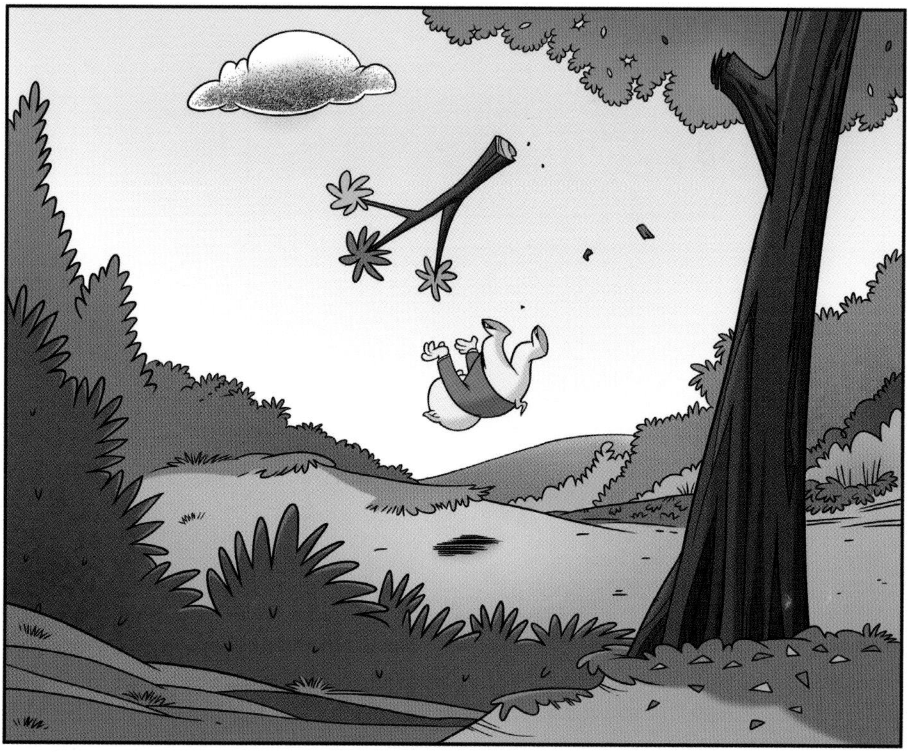

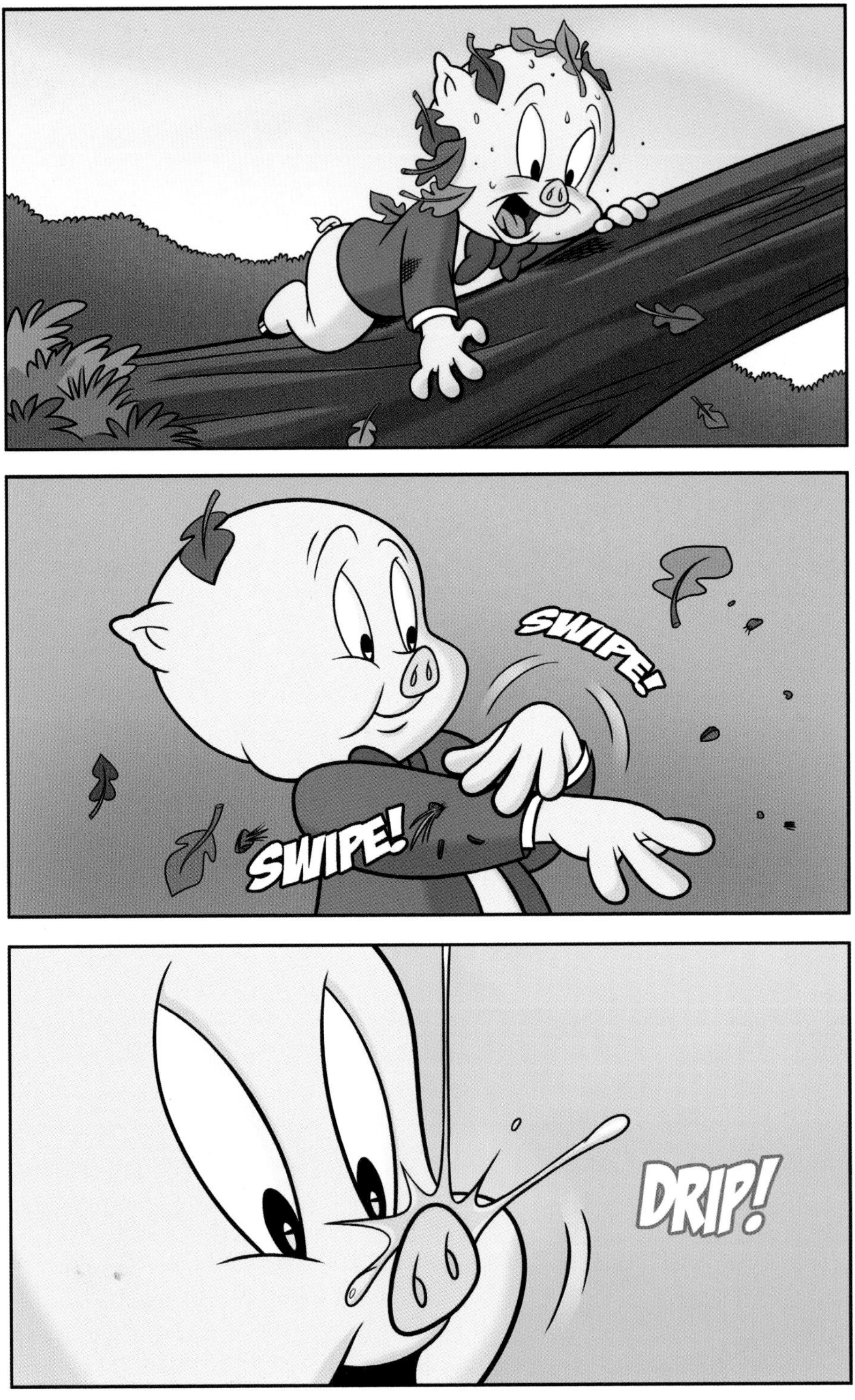

SWIPE!
SWIPE!
DRIP!

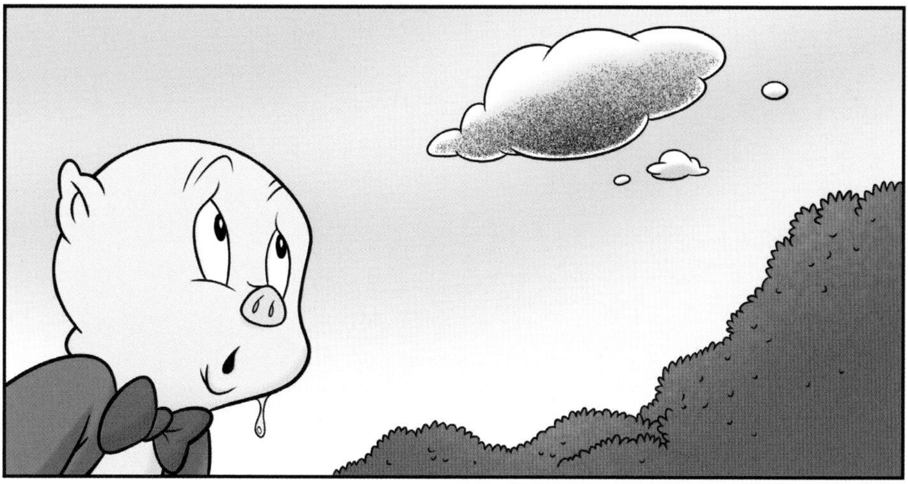

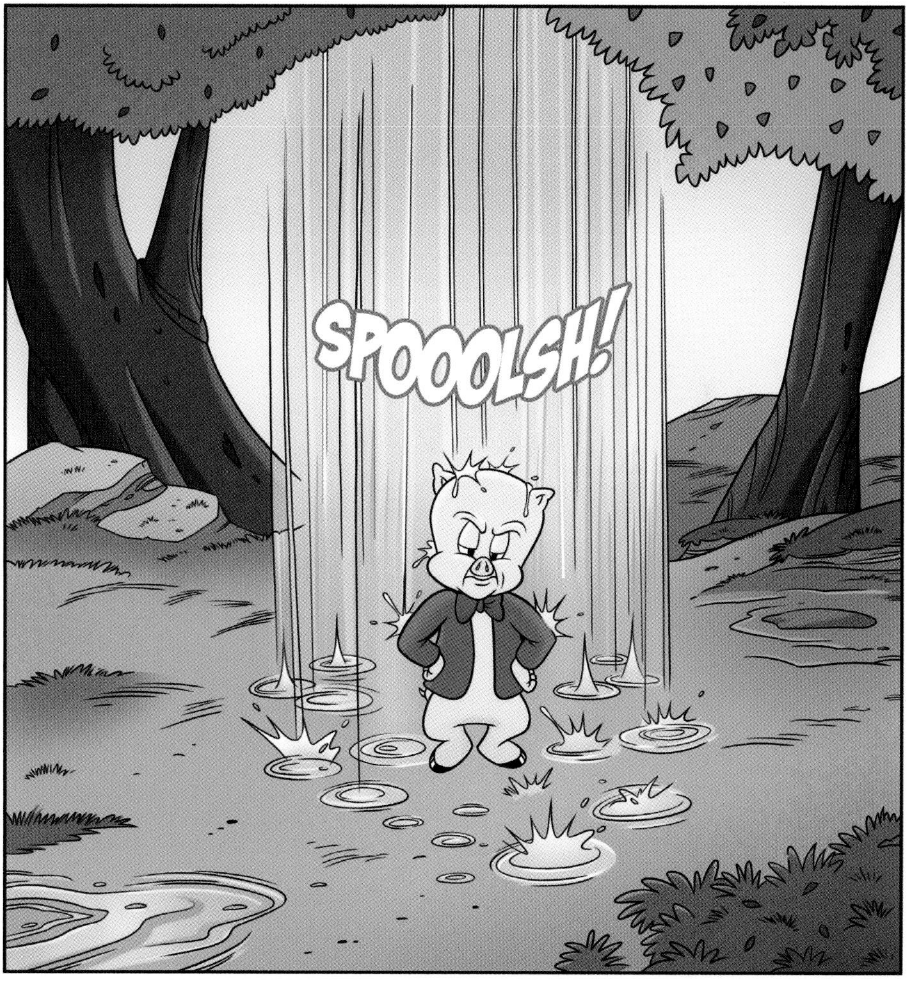
SPOOOLSH!

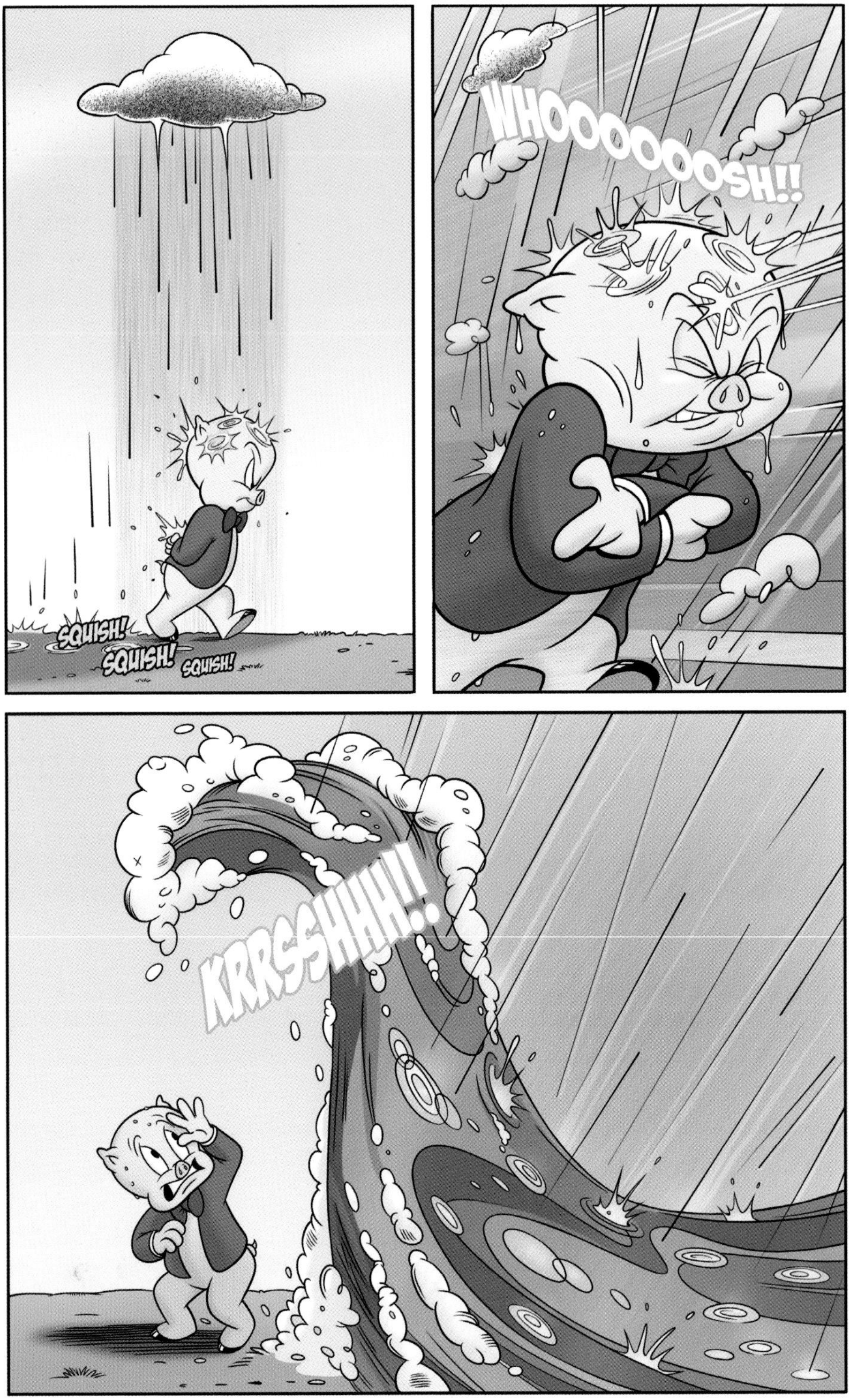
SQUISH!
SQUISH!
SQUISH!
WHOOOOOOOSH!!
KRRSSHHHH!!

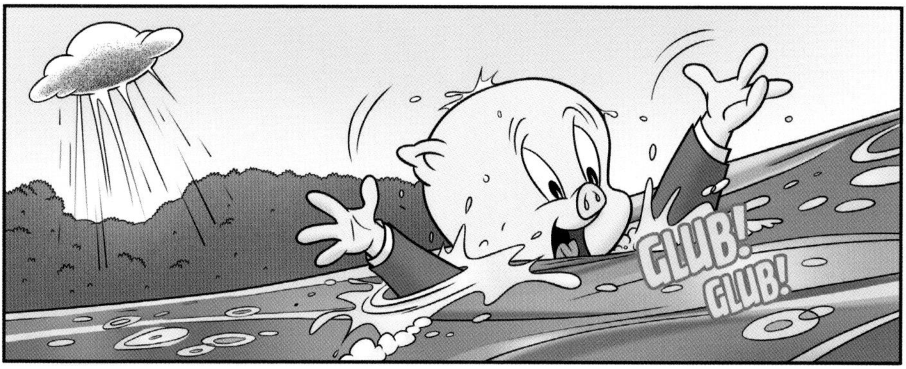
GLUB!
GLUB!

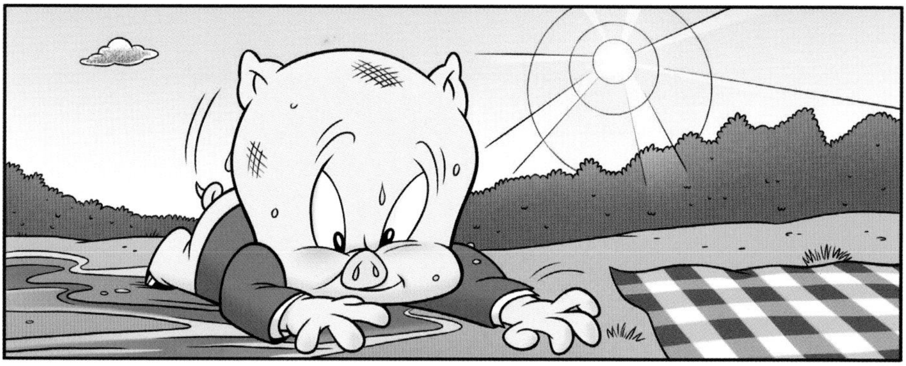

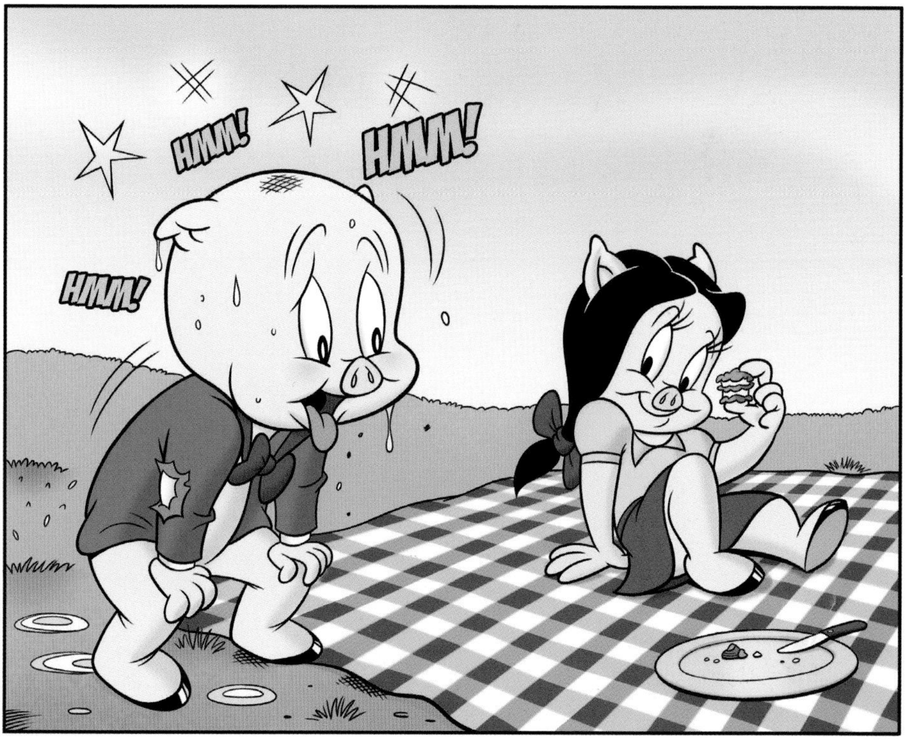
HMM!
HMM!
HMM!

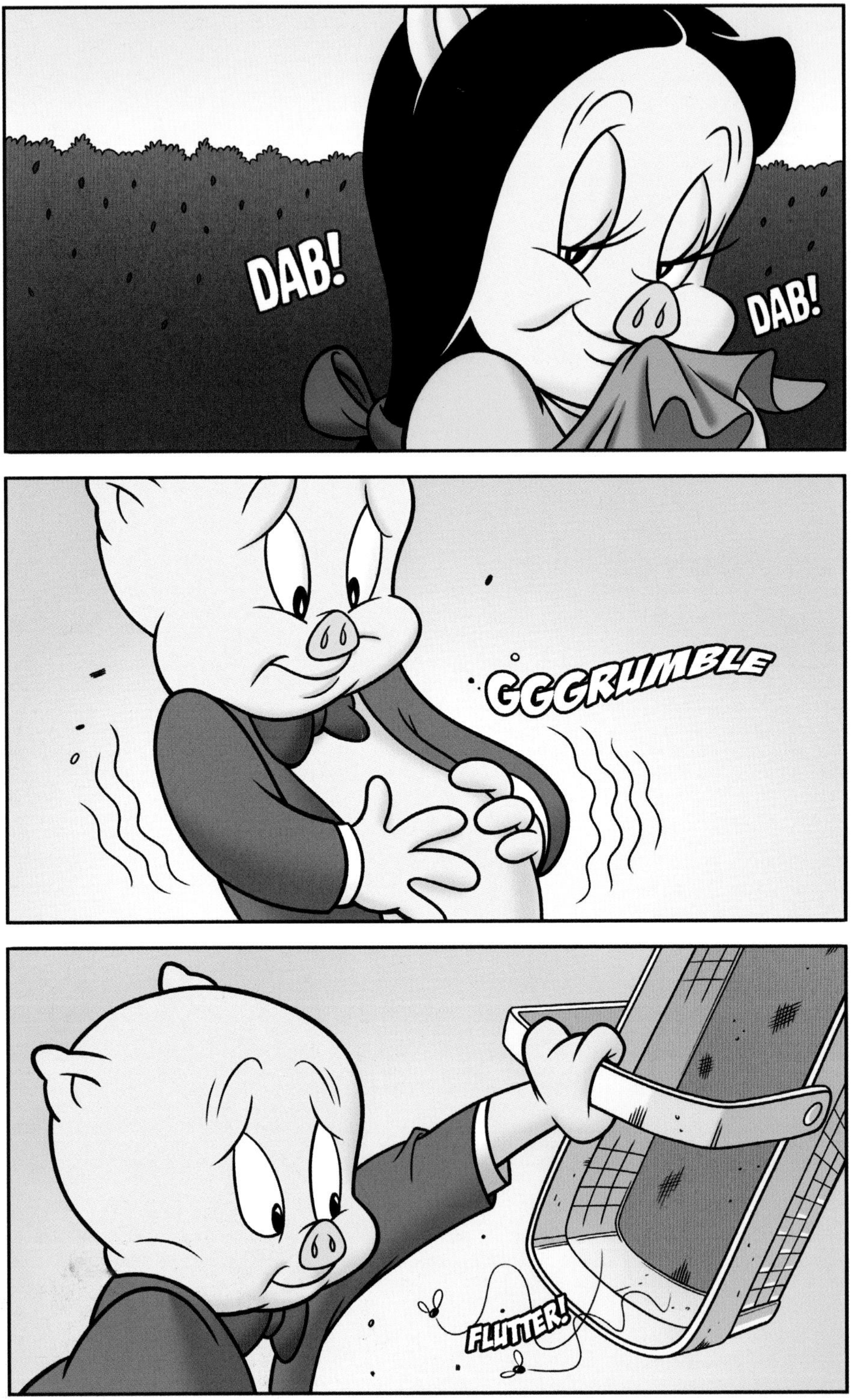
DAB!
DAB!
GGGRUMBLE
FLUTTER!

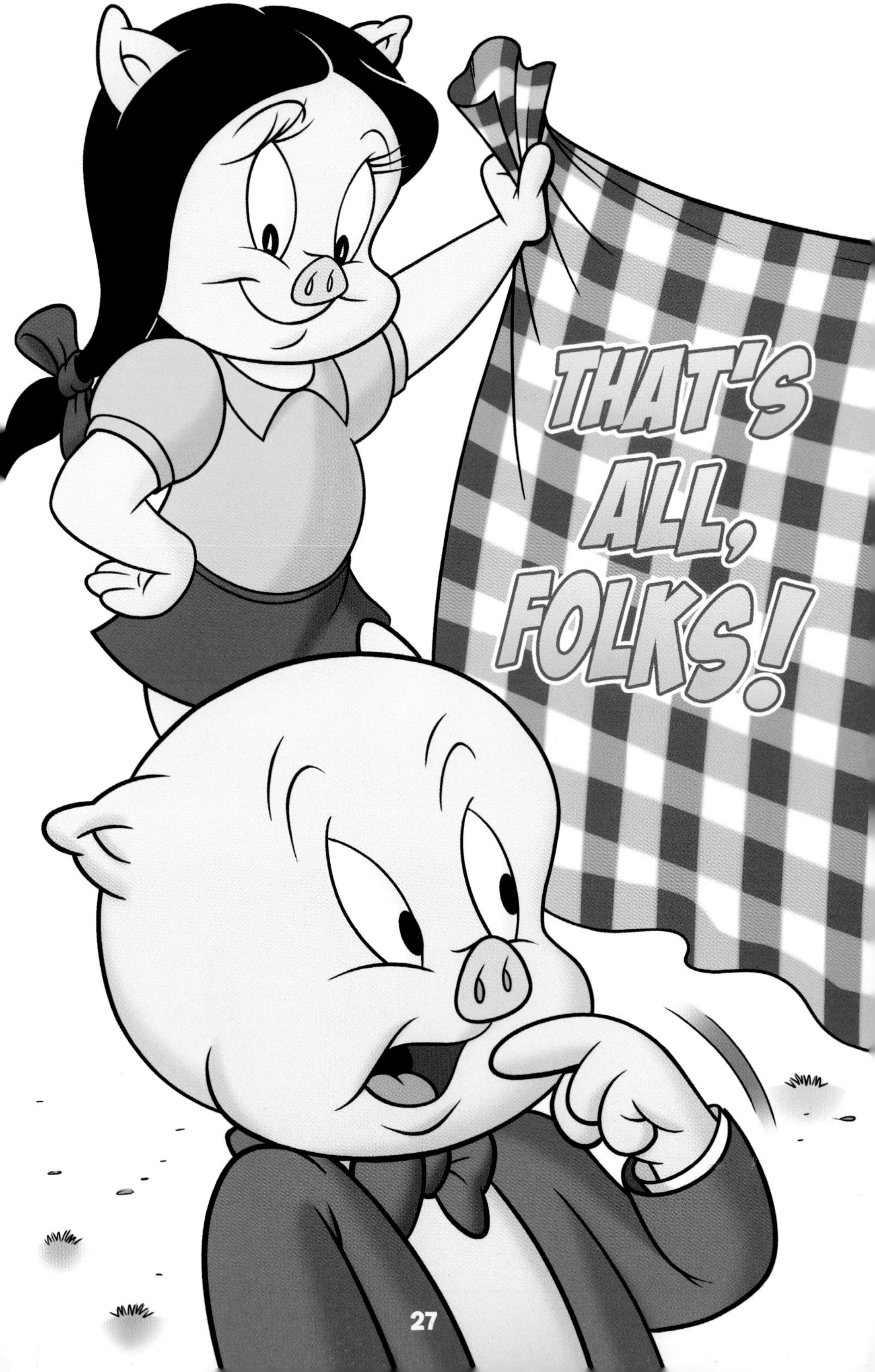
THAT'S ALL, FOLKS!

# Panel Talk

**1.** What do Porky and Petunia's hand gestures tell you in this panel?

**2.** Why does Porky have so many arms here? What is he doing?

SCRITCH!
SCRITCH!
SCRITCH!

3. What happened to Porky's sandwich? How do you know?

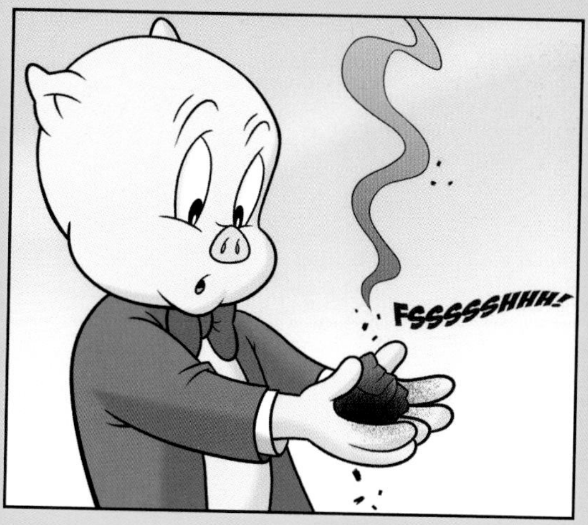
FSSSSSHHH!

4. How does Porky feel in this panel? What clues tell you that?

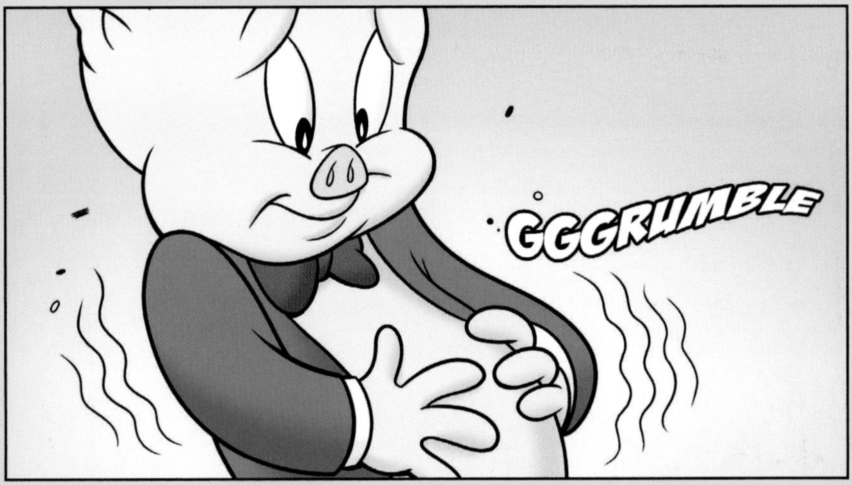
GGGRUMBLE

# LOONEY TUNES™

# Through the Years

Looney Tunes has entertained fans both young and old for more than 90 years. It all started back in 1930 with animated short films that ran in movie theaters. By 1970, these shorts leaped from big movie screens to small TV screens. From that point forward, generations of young fans have grown up watching these classic cartoons in their own homes.

What makes Looney Tunes so successful? Its amazing cast of characters, of course! Stars include Bugs Bunny, Porky Pig, Daffy Duck, Tweety, Sylvester, Marvin the Martian, Road Runner, and Wile E. Coyote. And don't forget their outrageous costars! Elmer Fudd, Yosemite Sam, Foghorn Leghorn, Pepé Le Pew, and the Tasmanian Devil add hilarious hijinks to every story.

With such a zany cast, it's no wonder Looney Tunes' return to the big screen often bursts beyond straight animation. Modern films have featured Bugs Bunny and his friends mixing things up with live-action sports and movie stars in *Space Jam* and *Looney Tunes: Back in Action*. And in 2021, the film *Space Jam: A New Legacy* has them destined for even more out-of-this-world adventures!

# About the Author

**Derek Fridolfs** is the #1 *New York Times* bestselling writer of the DC Secret Hero Society series, and the Eisner-nominated co-writer of the Batman Li'l Gotham series. He has worked in comics for more than 20 years as a writer, artist, and inker on a variety of beloved properties, including Looney Tunes, Scooby-Doo, Teen Titans Go, DC Super Hero Girls, Teenage Mutant Ninja Turtles, Adventure Time, Regular Show, and Disney Princess. Derek's recent graphic novels include *Batman Tales: Once Upon A Crime* and *Batman: Crack The Case*, and he is also the co-creator of the mythical adventure series Half Past Peculiar. He resides in California's central valley.

# About the Illustrator

When **Scott Gross** watched his first Looney Tunes cartoons as a child, they were already classics. He knew he was seeing something of quality from an earlier era that had stood the test of time and was still funny. Since then he's become the author and illustrator of many stories starring Bugs Bunny and the gang. In each one he strives to preserve the timeless characters and humor we have all grown to love.